De:

MW01050763

DEATH

IN

FULL

SWING

Death in Full Swing

Death in Full Swing

Water-Blood-Spirit Publishing

Book & Cover design copyright © 2018 by PAUL ISERI
Contact Website: contact@iseridesigns.com

Published in the United States of America

ISBN: 9781724178565

DEATH IN FULL SWING

Volume 1

By

Death in Full Swing

The day is off to a running start when Emma and Teddy Snow witness a murder in a park. Emma, a loveable smart-alec plays detective as she plays the town detectives with her friend, Arnie, while tracking down the killer.

–Rita Ariyoshi, Author, Honolulu Hawaii

"With a keen eye for clues and reconnaissance help by her trusty snowman, Emma Rae is definitely not your average 10-year-old in solving big crimes, don'tcha know! In between sips of hot cocoa and rides on her bike, she lives out dreams that for most kids ended when they turned off their televisions. D.V. Whytes offers intriguing and witty dialogue along with pastels of small-town America that hearken back to a simpler time. But as readers learn in this engaging series, things aren't always what they seem. And who says a pre-teen can't teach adults a thing or two about catching a killer!"

– Gary Robertson, journalist, North Carolina

Readers of all ages will love precocious young Emma and her plush pal, Teddy Snow as they unravel murder mysteries in small-town Austin, Minnesota. These fun, cozy short stories are filled with local color, and witticisms only a nine-year-old could supply.

- Laurie Hanan, author of fun Hawaiian mysteries

Death in Full Swing

Acknowledgements

With heartfelt gratitude, we thank the *Word Wranglers* for their efforts to make this a better book—Bob Newell, Thea Marshall, Gail Baugniet, Laureen Kwock & Joanna Bressler for all your help.

We are grateful for our wonderful parents who raised us right and saw fit to discipline us as needed.

A special thanks to Mom—Donna Whelan in helping us remember how things were in the sixties.

And finally, a heart full of gratitude for the life and friendship of Police Officer Duane Klingerman: Nine-David-Thirteen—a wonderful man and police officer, dedicated to his family, the children in his neighborhood and the townspeople of Austin Minnesota. Dec 29, 1924- Aug 14, 2018. He is missed and remembered fondly.

Death in Full Swing

The Town of Austin Minnesota,

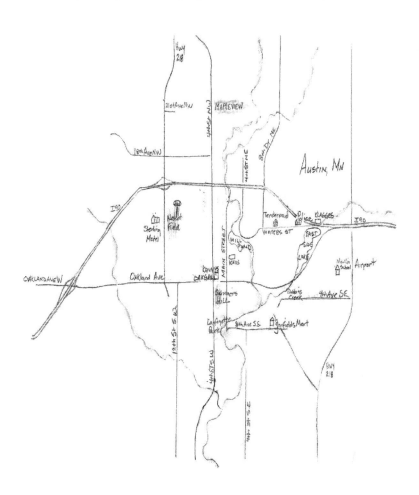

Death in Full Swing

LULLABIES OF LONG AGO

Butter pecan coated in chocolate and covered in candy sprinkles ... oh how yummy. It was a favorite of mine and the first taste is always the best. "Ummm ..." I murmured, eyes closed.

Detective Haugen firmly placed his hands on the picnic table where I sat, one on either side of me. Leaning forward, he said, "I'm glad you're feeling better Emma. Evidently ice cream works better than smelling salts."

I remained stoically calm, licking the melting

part before it reached my hand. Then, while picking off some of the sprinkles, I managed to say, "It's a pretty day though." Stalling was paramount, as far as I was concerned.

"Yes, Emma. It's nice out. Now tell me what you saw." The detective's questioning was steadfast, but he still seemed unaware of my ploy, at least as far as I could tell.

"Where's Teddy?" I looked around, half in a panic, my blonde ponytail swinging about.

"He's in my car."

I gave him a look of concern, and so he added, "He's fine. No one can get to him. Now, what did you see today?"

I knew he wasn't about to let up, but the ice cream was too good to abandon, even if, for only a moment. I figured I could get half of it down before telling him what he wanted to know. Smiling, I took a big bite from the top, my mouth now full of luscious goo.

"That's the last time I buy you a double dip," he said, deducing that this was going to take longer than he wanted. Impatiently, he sat down with a sigh, looked at his watch and crossed one leg over his other knee.

"What's the difference between being a detective or a police officer? Do you have to be a policeman before you can be a detective?"

But he wasn't buying it, and began to whistle, or at least tried to whistle. I started to feel sorry for him, and said, "I didn't see anything. It was Teddy Snow who saw it all."

"Teddy. Are you telling me I bought that ice cream for the wrong person?"

I froze. "Uh ... well, Teddy tells me everything."

"Okay. What did Teddy tell you? And aren't you a little old to be lugging a stuffed snowman around in the hot summer? How old are you anyway?"

"Almost ten, and for your information," I began, a little formally, "a snowman doesn't like ice cream. It would be like eating his buddy. Besides, you just don't understand."

The crew from the medical examiner's office was now lifting the old lady from the swing. They laid her gently on their gurney. I tried to watch from atop my perch, a short distance away. Most people think I'm too young for such things. But I fully intended to be a top notch investigator when I grow up.

Daddy told me there were over twenty thousand people living in Austin, Minnesota. Now that's a lot. And since Austin was such a booming metropolis, and, since I was planning to be the city's Sam Spade or Sherlock Holmes, then it was important for me to use every opportunity available. I had a lot to learn. Could I help it if fate put me in the right place at the right time?

"Don't look over there," the detective said. "Let's get back to what Teddy saw."

"Well, Teddy was on the merry-go-round. He likes to get a full view of everything and this way he could. I was lying down in that patch of dandelions over there." I pointed to a spot next to the bushes. "Did you know that if you hold one under your chin, your skin turns yellow ... that is of course, if you like butter. Do you like butter Detective Haugen?" I picked up a wilting weed lying next to me and waved it under his chin.

He rolled his eyes and I knew it was time to give him a little something and so I said, "I heard the squeak in the swings as it went back and forth. But Teddy was on the lookout, so I stayed where I was."

"That was probably smart. So what happened next?"

"Did I ever tell you about the night daddy brought Teddy home?"

"No, but that's not what's important, at least not now."

"Oh but it is. It's so very important. One night, when I was a little girl, daddy came in to kiss me goodnight. Before he left, he placed Teddy right next to me. That made me smile. You see, I love my daddy.

Then he tiptoed out of the room so he wouldn't wake me. He watched me all the way to the door ... he always does. When he closed it, I moved Teddy closer and fell asleep with him in my arms. He was so soft and fluffy.

Teddy remembers that night too. Did you know that he talks to me when I'm sleeping? And that night he said I warmed his heart."

"Wouldn't that be dangerous for a snowman?"

Ignoring his tease, I continued my story. "Well ... do you know what he did then? He kissed me just like daddy does. That's when the ball from the tip of his stocking cap flopped over and tickled my nose. I had to push it aside, so I wouldn't giggle.

"And why is this important?"

"Well, that night Teddy became my protector while I slept. And do you know what else? He knows lullabies from all over the world, and when I can't sleep, he sings to me."

"That's nice Emma. Why don't I just take you and Teddy Snow home?"

"But I thought you wanted to know what we saw."

Detective Haugen let out a sigh. He knew he was being played. "And what was that?"

With the ice cream gone, I wiped my mouth with a napkin. There are rules of etiquette that must be followed in society. Impressions are important, and I was not about to let the detective think I was uncouth.

"Well … my favorite one is an old Russian lullaby," and I began to sing to him, "*Sleep my baby, sleep my pretty, Bai-ush-ki bayu. While the moon is shining ..."*

"No, not the lullaby ..." he said, clearly frustrated. He stood up and started to walk over to the swing set, hands on his hips.

"Mormor Ohlson came by herself," I said, rather quickly. "Did you know that Mormor is what the Norwegians call a grandma?"

"Yes Emma, I have a Mormor [1] myself. And a Morfar [2]."

"Well, she just sat on that swing and started to cry."

"And that's what I got you an ice cream cone for?" He was getting a little miffed.

"After a little while, the paperboy came by. He sat on the swing next to her and they talked. His dog started to sniff around in the bushes—

---

[1] Mormor – Norwegian for grandmother
[2] Morfar – Norwegian for grandfather

over there where the wooded area begins" and I pointed to an area I considered creepy. "Mom told me never to go in there."

"That's right; you should stay in the open area. Who was the paperboy?"

"Teddy doesn't know. He said he never saw him before."

"Hmmm ..." Detective Haugen was taking notes now. He licked the tip of his pencil and scribbled something. "Go on ..." he said.

"Well his dog started to bark. And then this man with a hoodie came out. He threw rocks at the dog. Hit him too. I heard the poor thing yelp. The paperboy heard it too and called out to him. His name is News." I smiled and stuck out my chest, as if I had just unlocked a great secret.

"And then what happened?"

"The hoodie man saw Mormor Ohlson in the swing next to the paperboy."

"So what did he do?"

"He kicked the dog and ran towards them. The paperboy tried to get Mormor Ohlson up out of the swing, but I think she was too scared to move. Anyway, the hoodie guy grabbed the paperboy by his arm and hit Mormor on the head with that rock. The paperboy got loose and ran away. See, his papers are still in his bike basket over there, near the slide."

"Could you describe the paperboy to me?"

"I don't think so. And besides, Teddy doesn't know him."

"Did he see the face of the man with the hoodie?"

"Only his nose and mouth, the hoodie covered his eyes. I think I've told you everything detective. Are you going to take us home now?"

"Well, do you know what kind of dog it was? How big was it?"

"He came up to my knees and had dark brown fur. It was a little curly. Oh, and there was a white spot on his one eye." I touched my forehead with me finger, as if that added some kind of intellectual power and I added, "It was the left one."

And there it was. I had told him everything. Well almost everything ... all except for what I found under the swing. That was my news.

♪♪♪ ♪♪♪ ♪♪♪ ♪♪♪

That night, once Emma was fast asleep, Teddy began his nocturnal chat. He had more to say about what he saw that day in the park as well as what he saw from the police car. When Emma grew restless he began to softly sing an Old Icelandic lullaby to ease her back into Never-Neverland. *"Sleep my darling baby sleep; rain is gently falling. ..."*

Death in Full Swing

DO IT YOURSELF

Do it yourself ... that's my motto all right. If you want something done right, you need to it yourself. Besides, who else knows best how it should be done. At least that's what I was thinking when I woke up.

"Wow!" I said, and picked up Teddy. "What an exciting day we had yesterday. Now, don't worry. I made sure I put the stuff we found under the swing back in my pocket. We'll look at it later." I patted my dress on the right side. Teddy liked to be assured of things he couldn't see. As soon as I finished dressing, I tucked him under my arm and headed downstairs.

When I got to the kitchen, Mom had a bowl of Grape Nuts sitting on the table, along with a glass of orange juice. All she usually said was, *good morning* as I pulled my chair out, followed by *eat your breakfast*. Today wasn't any different.

I was half way to the bottom of the bowl when dad came in. He sat down and said, "Good morning Emma. I wanted to let you know that I talked to Detective Haugen last night."

"He's real nice. He bought me an ice cream."

"Yes, that's what I hear. He told us that you saw Mormor Ohlson get hurt."

"Killed daddy—she was killed."

Dad grunted and with lips tightened, looked over at Mom as if in search for help. She smiled back at him. I think there was a twinkle in her eye. With that she leaned against the kitchen counter and took a bite of her English muffin. I saw him squirm a little in his seat. Something was up.

"Well, your mother and I don't want you going back to the park until they find the man who did this."

"But he's not there anymore. Besides, that park is keen[3]."

After Mom gave Dad one of *her* looks, I got one from him. But who do I get to give a look? I bit my lip while thinking life was unfair and looked back towards Mom. Her arms were crossed and her eyebrows all crinkly.

Dad sighed. "Emma, you're a smart girl. But being gifted doesn't necessarily protect you from the evils of this world. You know that. Your mother and I understand your fondness to

---

[3] Keen - Neat, cool, groovy, nice

become a real gumshoe[4], but ..." and he paused here, his smile morphing into another one of his *looks* before continuing, "Let me make myself perfectly clear—you are not to go back there."

Hmmm, this wasn't going to be easy. "Yes," I said, but it was really more like a groan.

I got down from my chair and circled my foot on the floor, trying to figure out my next move. Then, as Dad took his first sip of coffee, I grabbed Teddy by the nose and ran out the kitchen door. Quickness was essential, at least before any more restrictions were made clear. Seeing an opening, I grabbed Teddy and bounded towards the door. A loud bang sounded as the screen door slammed shut. I hollered, "Bye. I'm going to Arnie's."

Three houses down, I stopped and hid behind a tree. After my breathing slowed down, I peeked around to see if they were looking for me. "Whew. That was a close call, wasn't it Teddy."

---

[4] Gumshoe - Detective

There was no time to lose and so I ran the rest of the way.

*** *** *** ***

I held five pebbles in my hand and tossed the first one. I hoped Arnie would be in his room. It clinked when it hit the window pane. I waited. No Arnie—so I tried again. Finally after the fourth pebble, he opened the window and stuck his head out. "Cut that out." He looked back inside and hollered, "I'm sorry Mom—it was the cat. She knocked something off my dresser." Looking back down he said, "I'm coming already."

"What took you so long?" I asked, as we started down the street.

"What's your hurry? Hey, where we going anyway?"

"Mormor's."

"That old lady's ... why?"

"Because she's dead, that's why."

"Dead?"

"As a doornail."

"How do you know?"

"Cause I saw her, that's why."

"I don't believe you."

"So, then ask Teddy."

"There you go again. You and that stupid stuffed snowflake—it's like he's your blankie, or something. You gonna suck your thumb too, little girl?" Arnie teased, as we stepped onto the swinging bridge.

Half way across, we stopped to watch the Cedar River flow. The wind was blowing, causing the bridge to sway a little. I tightened my grip on the rope.

"This is a good place to ditch that snowball,"

he said, and started across once again.

"You don't understand. Besides, he's not bothering you. Just leave us alone."

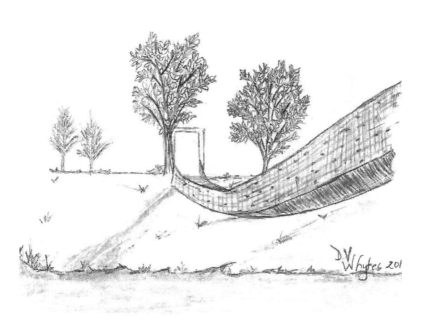

"Good, then I don't have to go to the old lady's then."

"Yes you do."

"Who's gonna make me?"

"Now who's the baby?"

"Not funny," he said, and tossed the stick he had been carrying into the river.

••• ••• ••• •••

All was quiet when we reached Mormor Ohlson's place. Just in case someone was watching, we marched proudly up to the front door and knocked. After a short moment, I hollered as if responding to a request, "Okay, we'll meet you there," and we jumped from the porch and went along the side of the house and into the backyard.

"Whew," Arnie said, and wiped his forehead. "No attack dogs."

I rolled my eyes and started to look under

things ... the doormat, a potted plant, an empty
cooler and last of all … a cardboard box. But
there was no key. I pulled the chair over and
reached to the top of the window sill. I saw that
in a movie once, but still, no key. So I opened the
screen door and grabbed the doorknob. It was
open. I smiled and Arnie said, "Nifty[5]."

Carefully, I positioned Teddy Snow next to
the plant, so he could spy on what was going on.
Then I waved for Arnie to follow.

We walked in, "Anybody home?" I hollered,
just in case there was somebody there. But no
one answered back.

The windows lacked curtains, which made
the kitchen bright. Dirty dishes filled the sink, a
cup of cold coffee lay on the table along with soft
butter and a slice of half eaten toast. There was a
dish under the table with what looked like mashed
potatoes smooshed around. The newspaper was

---

[5] Nifty –cool, great.

open and there was a coffee stain and a pencil mark in the middle of it. A good investigator needed to notice all these little clues. I grabbed the page and folded it into a small square and stuffed it into my pocket along with my newfound trinket.

Arnie was already in the living room and called back, "What are we looking for?"

"Something that tells us what she was doing yesterday, or even who she was."

"She was old lady Ohlson," he hollered back.

I snuck a peek in the refrigerator. "Yuk ... broccoli." Once past the bad stuff, I noticed some lefsa[6] and lutefisk[7]. Lutefisk by the way is way-yuk ... she needs to throw the stinky stuff away. Besides, anybody with half a mind knows that the only thing that goes with lefsa is butter and sugar.

---

[6] Lefsa – Norwegian tortilla made with mashed potatoes
[7] Lutefisk – Scandinavian air-dried white fish or salted and .
treated with lye and it has an extremely pungent odor

There wasn't much else in the fridge, but I did notice a container that looked like it had rotten ick inside. It was way in the back on the bottom shelf. I wasn't about to open it and shivered as my eyes ran past the lutefisk again.

Before I could decide that there was nothing important in here, I had to open the crisper drawer. That's when I noticed a big wad of newspaper lying under some lettuce, carrots, rhubarb and apples. My curiosity was peeked and as I pulled at the paper, a gun rolled out from underneath. I was totally flabbergasted. Quickly, I wrapped it up, placed it back where I had found it and slammed the fridge door. My heart was pounding faster than ever.

It was time to see what Arnie was up to. But before I could move a muscle, he came running in, "It's the cops. We gotta go."

"No, it's too late. We'll have to hide inside."

He ran into the hallway and I started to

follow, but stopped short. I thought I'd better bring it with me. Who knows what would happen if Detective Haugen found the gun. Mormor was always real nice to me. I didn't want him to think she was a fugitive or something. So I opened the fridge, and carefully pulled out the pistol and went to look for Arnie.

Dad believed in his right to bear arms and he knew it his sworn duty to make sure his children were knowledgeable in the proper use and danger of any weapon. He always said, "It's hatred that hurts another person, so check your heart first."

At least once a week he spent time showing me how to hold a knife or gun. He gave me regular lectures to be sure I was fully convinced that playing with them was foolish and dangerous.

To prove this fact, he took me out to the country. We stood in a big empty field and he held my hand tightly against the pistol grip. We aimed it together and shot at a tree. The noise hurt my ears and the recoil pushed me backwards

… I fell into daddy's arms. These sessions gave me a great respect for all forms of weapons.

"Over here," Arnie called out.

He was halfway up the attic ladder when I reached him. Once I followed him up, I helped him pull at the rope in order to raise the ladder. The opening automatically closed once the ladder was raised.

Detective Haugen picked Teddy Snow up. He had already searched the home and was about to check the backyard and porch. He chuckled. She must have watched us through the window and left without the toy, he thought. Maybe she's out here hiding. "Emma, Emma you left Teddy. If you don't come to get him, I'll have to book 'em at the station." But there was no response.

Up in the attic Emma whispered, "Don't worry Teddy, I'll come get you.

Death in Full Swing

DON'T CHA KNOW

Arnie and I descended from the attic once the police had driven away. We spent the rest of the morning looking through Mormor Ohlson's belongings, but it didn't help much. There simply was nothing to go through. In other words, the cupboards were bare and the walls too. It made me feel odd.

There were no pictures of family and friends sitting around, no flowers or knickknacks of any kind and the junk drawers were nearly empty as well. I searched her dresser drawers and closet, pushing the shoes aside to see if there was anything in the back. I even stood on a stool to look in the medicine cabinet. And then, in a moment of silly frustration, I peeked under the rug and saw a black smudge. I turned it over and imagine my surprise, when I realized that the smudge was a number. *What could this mean*, I wondered and copied it on the hem of my dress.

Arnie crawled under the bed, stuck his hand between the mattress and box springs, and looked under the sofa and chairs. Finally, he said, "This is dumb. Besides, it's time for me to go home. Mom will be looking for me, don't cha know[8]."

"You're just hungry," I said. And then, as if on cue, my stomach let out a low rumble.

---

[8] Don't cha know – you know this

Arnie giggled.

"You go on," I said. "I'll be right behind you." I went back into the bedroom to get a box of loose photos that I had found in the attic. I returned to the refrigerator and placed the gun inside the box, underneath the pictures, on the bottom.

♪♪♪ ♪♪♪ ♪♪♪ ♪♪♪

When I got home, I ran straight to my bedroom and hid the box with the gun behind a loose board in my closet. Then I set my shoes back in front of it. This was my favorite hiding place. I stood there feeling a little proud of myself and then went to the kitchen for lunch.

I was starved, but had to get moving. It seemed like I couldn't eat fast enough. So I stuffed the last of my peanut butter and strawberry jelly sandwich in my mouth, jumped off my chair and opened the back door. "Mort and I are going for a ride," I hollered, running out the door. As I headed towards the garage, I took that last bite of PB and J[9], wishing for some milk to wash it down.

I pulled Mort out from behind the garden hose, jumped on the pedals, and headed off to find Detective Haugen. I named my bike Mort for several reasons. One, its short for the Latin word mortem, which makes me think of dead bodies. I do plan on investigating murders, so it seemed to fit. It also rhymes with court, which makes sense too. And then again, I just like the name.

Once I arrived at the police station, I had to persuade the dispatcher to let me through the door into the inner sanctum of the police world. Her name was Donna. She used to babysit me and I really liked her. She has a boyfriend too. His name is Tommy and she gets all red in the face when I mention him ... yucko schmutz[10].

"Are you and Mort here to get Teddy

---

[9] PB and J - Peanut Butter and Jelly
[10] Yucko Schmutz – icky, nasty, unacceptable

Snow?" she asked.

"How did you know?"

"Detective Haugen told me you'd be here. So, why were you snooping around Mormor Ohlson's place?"

"So where's Teddy then?" I asked, hoping to escape the last question. Donna gave me a stern look as she held the door open. I walked through beneath her outstretched arm, smiling.

"I'll let Haugen know you're here," she said. But quickly, before she dialed the number, I placed my left hand over the round dial on the phone and put my right index finger in front of my pursed lips to mimic a *shhh*, adding, "Don't tell him."

"But he's got questions for you," she said, in a sing-songy voice.

I shuffled my foot on the floor again. I'm not sure how this little movement helps me think, but it hasn't let me down yet. I pushed out my lower lip in a pout, hoping it would add some *umph* to my plea for her to keep quiet on the subject of my whereabouts.

"You're gonna get me in trouble someday," she said, and pulled Teddy from a file cabinet drawer. *Darn, there's not much he could have seen cooped up in there,* I thought.

I smiled, grabbed Teddy by his arm and proceeded to do the *I've got to go potty* dance." It's quite an effective method that lets me roam places when no one else is looking.

"Around the corner and to your left. Don't be long, or I'm coming after you," Donna said, with a sigh.

She opened a back door for me and I heard her groan as I walked through. I took a left as directed and then, when I thought she was no longer watching, turned around and ran off in the opposite direction. Detective Haugen's office was just around the corner. The voices were fairly easy to hear since his door was open. I scrunched down to listen.

"This is strange indeed. There are no records of any Addie Ohlson, seventy-two, before she moved here, about ten years ago."

Another voice said, "And from what I can tell, the old lady kept to herself. But three days ago she called the precinct late at night. She thought someone was snooping around her place."

Hmmm … who was Detective Haugen talking to?

"Was a uniform dispatched to check it out?" Haugen asked.

"Ja[11], but they didn't find anything. I'll go back and have another look."

Oh ... I knew that voice; it was Officer Klingerman, who I also knew fondly by his call

---

[11] Ja – Norwegian word for *yes*, pronounced ya

letters; Nine David Thirteen. I called him that often. He was tall with some gray hair above his ears and had what he lovingly referred to, as his donut belly-basket. I really liked him. He could hit a baseball farther than anyone else and had a smile that never ended.

"And while you're at it," Haugen said, "ask around; see if you can find out who her paperboy was."

A chair dragged across the floor. Uh, oh ... I thought, and held my breath.

The detective asked, "Come to think of it, did we ever ID the hoodie guy Emma told us about?"

"No, and we still don't have a description. We haven't had any other complaints either. I'll double check the park as well, just in case."

"You think he was the one snooping about Ohlson's place the other night?"

"That'd be my guess."

The toe of one of Klingerman's shoes poked out the door. I did a quick about face and ran smack into Donna. Her hands rested on her hips and she had daggers in her eyes.

I offered a weak smile.

"Haugen," Donna said. "You've got company."

Klingerman stepped out. He put his hand behind me and gently pushed me through the door. I stiffened my resolve and held Teddy high. With a big smile on my face, I said, "Gee thanks Detective Haugen. Where did you find him?"

Haugen pushed his glasses down his nose to peer at me from over the top.

Nervously, I continued, "I wouldn't have slept a wink without him. You weren't gonna try to take him home to see if he'd tell you things while you slept, were you?" I turned to make sure Donna had left. I knew I was gonna hear about this again.

But then again, the detective was just as determined to get answers too, "What were you doing at Addie Ohlsons, Emma?"

There goes my foot again, moving about in circles. Hmmm ... "I just wanted to thank you for the ice cream yesterday."

But he didn't say a word and continued to stare at me over those glasses.

Arnie and I were just walking around. We saw your cars and wanted to see what was going on. I'd better be getting home. Me and Mort'll take Teddy with us. See you later." I bolted through the doorway, while Haugen hollered, "Emma ... Emma, wait.

Klingerman laughed as Haugen rolled his eyes, "At least you know where to find her."

♪♪♪ ♪♪♪ ♪♪♪ ♪♪♪

I gave up on finding Arnie and rode over to Skinners Hill—he wasn't in any of his usual spots. It's a great place to toboggan down in the winter time. I sighed as I looked up at the green grass, remembering the cold-weather fun.

I laid Mort down by the edge of the lagoon, at the bottom of the hill. Teddy was snuggly sitting in the basket that was attached to Mort's handle bars. I took my shoes off and waded in the cool, ankle deep water and began to think about all I'd seen and heard. That's when I stuck my hands in my pocket and felt the locket that I had found under the swing Mormor Ohlson had sat on. I had forgotten all about it.

As it lay in the palm of my hand, I marveled at the shiny locket with a gold rose on the front. I remembered how Teddy had said to make sure to look inside. He told me that it was important. He said it was the clue for our next move.

Sitting next to Mort now, I tried to open the charm, but it was stuck. So I pushed harder with my fingernail sticking into the crack. Finally it gave way. There were two pictures inside. On the left was a pretty lady who looked like Mormor must have looked a long time ago. On the other side was a little boy, a few years younger than me. Hmmm, he looks familiar, I thought.

A few big drops of rain plopped on my forehead and then my arms. I looked over at Teddy; his nose glistened from the drizzle.

Looking up at the sky, I saw dark clouds blowing in as heaven's tears wetted my cheeks. *Oh boy*, I thought. By the time Mort got us home, both Teddy and I were sopping wet.

....

Mom put Teddy in the dryer, ignoring my protestations and ushered me into the bathroom. She handed me a towel and started the bathwater.

"How about some hot cocoa when you're done?"

My pout immediately turned upside down, and into the tub I went.

Death in Full Swing

DOG EAT DOG

The next morning, the sun rays streaming through my window, woke me. I lay in bed for a little while contemplating all Teddy had told me last night. It was going to be a busy day. I checked my stash of secret odds and ends in the closet to make sure that the gun was still there. It was. When I pulled the necklace out, a few photos fell out of the box. One, in particular, caught my attention. It struck me as odd, but I wasn't sure why, so I stuffed it and the necklace in my pocket.

While brushing my teeth, I pondered the best way to tackle things before finally deciding to start my day at Mormor Ohlson's place. Teddy had said he'd seen the paperboy hiding in the bushes before the police had arrived. Mom was busy on the phone, so I snuck past and grabbed a donut on the way out.

Arnie's mom said he had already left for the day on his bike. Shucks ... it looked like I would have to go to Mormor's alone.

Before crossing the swinging bridge, Mort and I stopped at the park to place Teddy in a good look-out spot. I set him in a nook formed from a few tree branches where he could secretly watch the swing set area.

And then, once back up on the bridge, I took one last look to make sure he was okay. He didn't even notice I was checking on him. A small smile sneaked out while I watched him chat away with a squirrel. Secretly, I felt a little hurt. I guess I thought he'd be looking up to make sure

I was all right too. The day had hardly begun and already I had been let down twice; first Arnie and now Teddy. But I wasn't about to let a rough start slow me down. And so, with a stiff upper lip, Mort and I headed off to Mormor Ohlson's.

I found the back door open and all around, it was eerily quiet. I thought this seemed a little odd since I was sure Detective Haugen would have locked it. Scrunching down real low, I cracked the door barely enough to peek inside. Before I knew what was happening, I found myself pushed back on my haunches with wet all over my face. News was busy letting me know how happy he was to see me. "Blah!" I said, twisting my face sideways and trying to push him away.

"News, News ... get over here boy!"

Miraculously, the pup obediently retreated.

I found myself looking up at the newspaper boy, but I wasn't surprised ... I expected to find him here.

The lad stood there looking all sleepy and motioned for me to come in. It looked as though he had camped out in the house last night. His shoes and back pack lay on the floor and there were a few pillows on the couch.

"Who are you?" he asked, rather perturbed.

"Your new best friend."

He groaned.

"I know who you are," I said, triumphantly and maybe a little snotty-like too.

"What are you doing here? And how did you know Addie?"

"Shouldn't you be calling her Mormor? Because she was, wasn't she?" I was getting good at this.

"What makes you think that?" he asked, nervously. He turned away and opened the fridge. After pulling out a carton of grapefruit juice, he took a big swig and wiped his face with the back of his hand. In an effort to change the subject he asked, "You want some breakfast?" He slipped a slice of bread into the toaster and asked, "How'd you know anyway?"

"That's you, isn't it?" I asked, holding out the opened locket.

"Where'd you get that?" he asked, still a little edgy.

"Under the swing."

"Oh ..."

"The cops were here yesterday. They'll probably come back."

"They're not the only ones."

"You mean the hoodie guy?"

"You shouldn't be here." He opened the fridge again, then the crisper, grumbling as he searched in vain.

"It's not there."

"The cops take it?"

"No, I did."

"You're too little for that—you'd better give it to me," the paperboy demanded.

"Why was she crying?"

"What?"

"Why was she ..."

"It's none of your business." The toast popped up and he spread some peanut butter on it. He leaned against the counter and took a bite. "Where is it?"

"You're not old enough either," I said, firmly with my hands on my hips. Mom always did that when she meant business.

"Yes, I am. Seventeen in a month. Besides, I've had training. Now where is it?"

We heard a car drive up and park. I looked out the window and exclaimed, "It's Klingerman."

"What's a Klingerman?"

"Fast—we gotta hide."

The newspaper boy grabbed his gear and the collar around News's neck. I pulled the rope hanging from the ceiling to bring the ladder down. We scurried up, him carrying News and then quickly, raised the ladder.

News rested near the boy's gear while we peeked out the small attic window. Officer Klingerman searched all over the yard and in the garage. He picked up something from under a window. We couldn't tell what it was.

When Klingerman entered the house, the newspaper boy pulled News on his lap to keep him quiet. We couldn't watch the officer now, anyway. There was no way of knowing what he was up to, but he sure was taking his sweet time.

"Uh oh, the pillows," I said, than I clamped my hands over my mouth.

A few minutes later, we heard static and a garbled noise. Then, after a moment of silence, Klingerman said something, but it was all muffled. News let out a low growl. But thankfully the officer must not have heard, because he left right through the back door. We watched as he got back into his patrol car. He sat inside writing and talking on his radio before he finally left.

I imagined him calling it in; *Nine David thirteen ... all clear at Mormor's."* "Whew," I said, in relief and wiped my forehead. I felt like I had held my breath the entire time. I hadn't though. I mean I'm good, but, not that good.

Once back out of the attic, I looked around. I'm sure Officer Klingerman had noticed the toast and peanut butter, as well as the water dish on the floor. But if he knew we were here, then why, I wondered, did he leave?

"We gotta go," the newspaper boy said. He stuffed his gear into a bag, grabbed the toast and carton of juice. Then, as if on second thought, he went straight to the fridge and pulled out a tub of mashed potatoes and some cooked hot dogs. Giving a hotdog to News, he held the door open and nodded for me to vamoose. "You don't know me ... okay?"

"You're right. What's your name?"

"Bernie, and that's not what I mean."

"I know what you mean."

"Don't come back here."

Boy, people really like to tell you where you can't go, I thought. "But where will I find you?"

"You won't." And he was off, the dog trotting behind him.

I ran over to the neighbors fast, where I had hidden Mort and hopped on him so we could follow Bernie.

When we caught up, all he said was, "Bug out[12], why don't cha."

"Where are you going?"

"None of your business."

"Where's your Mom?"

"Don't have one ... anymore."

He started across the swinging bridge.

"You gonna sleep at Mormor's again?"

"Didn't I tell you to get lost?"

We both stopped short. Klingerman was in the park and looking all around. "Uh oh ..." I said.

"What?"

"He's getting awful close to Teddy, that's all."

---

[12] Bug out - Get out of here, go away, scram

"Whose Teddy?"

"My partner. You better beat feet[13]," I said. "He's looking for you. I'll go stall him."

Bernie and News did an about-face and I started back across the bridge.

---

[13] Beat feet - Scram, get lost, go away

Death in Full Swing

JA SURE, YOU BETCHA

Mort and I flew down the hill, bouncing at each
bump we met. "Yoohoo," I hollered, the wind
tossing my ponytail. I had successfully diverted
Officer Klingerman and was feeling full of
myself. Between that, the box of photos, and the
locket, I had guessed right. Bernie was Mormor
Ohlson's grandson. But then, all of a sudden, I
stopped.

The jolt of recent events replaced my smile

with a pout. I got off Mort and wheeled him over to a tree. Leaning him against it, I took my position in front of Teddy, who was calmly resting in the basket.

"Wait one minute," I said, a little loudly, shaking my finger in a scolding manner. Looking Teddy in the eye, I continued, "What happened to his Mom and why hasn't he ever visited the old lady before? Who's the hoodie guy and who would want to hurt old lady Mormor?" I realized there were still a whole lot of questions to answer. It was way too soon to celebrate. I needed to find the hoodie guy—but where to look?

*** *** *** ***

"You sure could get in a whole lot of trouble if your dad ever found out," Arnie said, while I was looking around in the bushes near the swing.

It had taken me longer to convince Arnie to go back to the park with me, than it had been to find him. He had been right where I thought he'd be all along—at the ball park hitting balls. "You gonna help me or not?" I asked.

"So what are we looking for now?"

"A brain for you," I said, sarcastically.

"Whoa, it's your dad!" Arnie exclaimed.

"Ja sure ... you betcha[14]."

"No, really. Look!"

My head popped up. Every nerve in my body on fire, but there was no one around. "Where?"

Arnie laughed. "Gotcha."

I stepped out from the bushes, with a smile. "Found it."

"Found what?"

"A key on a ring with a card attached. On the card, it says The Sterling Motel, that's what. Come on, let's go."

---

[14] You betcha – You better believe it

"Go where?"

"The Sterling Motel."

Arnie groaned.

"Oh don't be such a doofus[15]. Besides, we've got our bikes." And fifteen minutes later, we were hiding them behind the Sterling Motel.

"What a dive," Arnie muttered.

"The card on the key ring says Four-A."

Arnie peeked into the window once we found the room and said, "Nobody's inside."

Arnie put the key in the lock and in we went. The room was dark and dirty. I closed the curtains, so no one would know we were there.

He started looking under the bed, in the closet and bathroom. He liked crawling under things, but not me. I looked at the trash on the table. Yucko! There were McDonalds bags and

---

[15] Doofus – dumby'

crumpled wrappers, near-empty coffee cups, several squashed Coke cans, smushed ketchup packets and cold french fries on the table and floor.

But this time it was Arnie who found the prize. He pulled out a big envelope from between the mattress and box springs. We both plopped on the bed and he emptied the contents between us. Inside were recent pictures of Mormor Ohlson and her house as well as older pictures, ones when she was younger. In one picture she posed in front of Big Ben. She wore a tight fitted jacket with lots of buttons down the front, a full skirt, high heels and big brimmed hat. She was real pretty.

There was another one, a close up, that caught her looking in her purse. And, if you looked real hard, it appeared as though there might have been a gun inside. I took another look at the picture of her with Big Ben. There was someone in the background who looked familiar

... The following was written on the back of that picture. It said, *1943. Delays make deadly ends. Finish what's started. It ends here, at any cost.*

"Wow," I said. "1943, that's real ancient."

Deeply focused on our find, I jumped out my skin when I heard a noise outside.

Arnie said, "Someone's coming."

Duh.

Arnie rushed into the bathroom and jumped onto the toilet seat. I entered as he was climbing through. Halfway out, he reached for my hand. "Hurry up," he said.

Once safely outside, we squatted beneath the window. I was all keyed up and found it hard to keep my breathing quiet.

Inside the room, someone moved about noisily. The phone rang and with a grunt, a man answered it. "Ja ...," he said, "Nah, she's toast ... safe enough ... nah, she's the only one who knew

... a rock ... tossed it ... a boy and his dog ... give me a day ... don't think so ... tomorrow ... it's a small town."

A moment later the door slammed. Arnie looked around the corner, "It's the hoodie guy," he said, looking back at me for a second. "He's lugging a bag over his shoulder and heading for Wescott Field. We gotta tell Detective Haugen," Arnie exclaimed, before hopping on his bike. "Come on, let's go." Clearly he was excited.

"What? And tell him we were in the park and broke into a motel room? I'll be grounded forever."

"You want to follow him then?"

"Don't need to. He'll be back. He's probably going to the park or old lady Mormor's. Besides, Bernie's not there anymore."

"Who's Bernie?" Arnie asked.

Ignoring him, I jumped on the bike. Mort

and I headed down the road. "Come on ..." I hollered, "We've got work to do."

We stopped at Garfield's Groceries and left our bikes leaning against the two cement steps that led to the main door. It was hot, so the glass door was propped open with a brick. I pushed the screen door and walked inside. A fan blew cool air towards the counter, but I paid it no mind. I was too busy studying the new jars of candy next to the cash register.

"Ah ... why it's Miss Emma and Arnie," Mr. Nygaard said, as the screen door slammed behind us. "And yust vhat are de two of du up to today?" The old man's blue eyes twinkled. His white fluffy hair tousled from the wind of the fan. He leaned over the counter and gave me a big wink.

"A root beer slush please," Arnie said, while I ogled the candy jars.

"One for you too, Emma?"

"Yes, thank you Mr. Nygaard. When did you

get these big jars?"

"Oh, dese?" he asked, as if he were surprised to see them there. "Ja, dey are new." He was leaning forward now, his elbows on the counter. "Here, try one of dees[16] sveets for me. I vant to make sure dey[17] are good. Can't be accused of selling bad candy now, can I?"

---

[16] Dees – The word *these* with a Norwegian accent
[17] Dey – The word *they* with a Norwegian accent

Wow. I tried not to sound too eager, and said,

"Oh, uh, sure. But don't tell Momma. She might think you're trying to ruin my supper."

Gosta chuckled and opened the jar. He held it out for Arnie and me to reach inside.

"Did you hear about old Mormor Ohlson?" Arnie asked, before he popped a jawbreaker into his mouth.

By this time, I had taken my first sip of root beer slush. Ooh, the cold got caught in my throat and it hurt a bit—but tasted yummy.

"Oh such a terrible, terrible thing," he shook his head. I thought I saw a tear in his eye before he asked, "And how is it that du know about dis?" He gave Arnie and me a stern look.

Arnie was so excited over the slush and free candy that he began babbling his flap jaw[18] like a ditz[19]. "Emma saw her get killed and then we

---

[18] Flap jaw - Busy body, talks non-stop, gossip

found out that the newspaper guy is really her grandson. She was a real Mormor. And this hoodie guy ... well he hit her and he's looking for him too. And then ... then Emma found this ... this gun in her house ..."

I froze and gave Arnie my best death-stare. His eyes popped out of his head and his hand flew to his mouth. "Oh ... oh ..." he muttered.

Mr. Nygaard looked back and forth at me and Arnie. He gave a big sigh and said, "How about I call du Momma, let her know du bairn[20] are having dinner vith me?"

We just stood there looking at him.

"Ve vill have hot dogs and macaroni and cheese. Dat's of course, unless you prefer peanut butter and jelly?"

"Hot dogs," we both sang out in harmony.

---

[19] Ditz - Idiot, dummy, dork

[20] Bairn – Norwegian for *child/children*, pronounced bear-n

He walked over, shut the door and placed the closed sign out. "Komme[21] vith me," he said, and we walked to the back of the store.

---

[21] Komme – Norwegian for come, pronounced come-ah

LOTSA DIRT

Gosta was not able to sleep that night, and therefore was late opening the store. As was his routine, he walked over to the Ansafone [22] and clicked it on. While the machine rewound the tape, he unlocked the door and changed the sign to open.

Beep—he heard as the machine started to rattle off its messages: *Gosta, I need you to deliver a pound of coffee, and a dozen eggs. Gotta run— Time to trade is on, don't cha know*

---

[22]Ansafone - Name of an answering machine

... Again a beep and then—*Gosta, du gamla fuddy blindgångare* ... Oh no, not again, Gosta thought as Mrs. Gufstafsson's complaint continued. It was quickly followed with the noise from a phone being slammed down and

then another beep—*Mr. Nygaard, this is Emma.
Teddy figured it all out, we've got a plan. We're
on our way to the park. Meet us there as soon as
you can ...*

*Plan ... vhat plan? Yust vhat is Emma up to
now*, he wondered? Anxious, he rewound the
message. But the only additional information he
noticed was that the message was left at eight
thirty that morning. Looking at his watch he saw
that it was already twelve past nine. There was no
time to lose. He locked the store and headed
down the street. It would take him at least ten
minutes to get to the park.

♪♪♪ ♪♪♪ ♪♪♪ ♪♪♪

Arnie and I left our bikes by the swings and sat
down on the merry-go-round. I picked up my feet
before he gave it a little push. Once he climbed
on, we sat in the middle and started to go through
the pictures, one at a time.

"I bet old lady Mormor was a spy," Arnie

said, and put the photo back in the box.

"I think I'm getting dizzy," I said, with a close-up photo in one hand and holding the merry-go-round bar with the other.

Arnie stopped the ride and I stood to shake the woozies[23] from my head. I picked-up another picture, the one where she stood in front of Big Ben. That someone caught in the background surely looked familiar. I'm sure I knew who it was, but I wasn't ready to tell anyone yet.

"Why are we here?" Arnie asked, climbing on one of the merry-go-round bars.

"We're waiting for Bernie."

"Why?" he asked again, this time hanging upside down from the bar.

"Because, I've got some questions for him," I said, rather matter-of-factly.

─────────────────────────

[23] Woozies – Dizzy, confused, muddled

"Like what?"

"That had to be his Mom's picture in the locket. I think she died."

Feeling uncomfortable with the topic at hand, Arnie changed the subject. "I like Mr. Nygaard. That ice cream sundae was the best."

"Ja, and he sure asked a lot of questions last night. He was really upset about Mormor Ohlson. It got me thinking."

"Well, I hope you talked it over with that stuffed snowflake of yours."

I just smiled. Of course we had talked about it.

"Well, well. What do we have here?" It was the hoodie guy. He pushed the merry-go-round and it started spinning a little too fast. I held on tight.

Arnie had fallen off the ride since he was still upside down when it started spinning. I heard him hit the ground with a thud and a big *oof.*

"Where is it?" he demanded.

"Arnie," I shouted. But he didn't move. "Arnie," I called again. My fingers tightened as the merry-go-round continued to spin. My head turned left and then right, so I could keep my eyes on my friend.

"Aw, looks like your little buddy got an ouwie. Isn't that just too bad? And you're next if you don't hand it over."

"What did old lady Mormor ever do to you?" I cried, "You big meanie." I had to get off of this ride; it was making me sick to my stomach and besides, I couldn't think.

"You bozo[24], you can just eat dirt[25] for all I care," I hollered, before I stuck my tongue out. And it worked too. He got so mad he stopped the merry-go-round as soon as I was about to pass

---

[24] Bozo – Idiot, clown
[25] Eat dirt – result from putting your foot in your mouth

him by again. He grabbed me by my arms.

It was then that I saw Mr. Nygaard behind the hoodie guy. He placed his finger in front of his pursed lips, and then snuck over to Arnie. He shushed him, before helping him get behind the bushes, keeping his eyes on me the whole time. I saw Mr. Nygaard whisper to Arnie and point up the street. Arnie nodded and ran off in that direction.

"I said, hand it over! Now!" The hoodie guy was mad and wouldn't stop shaking me. I felt like a milk shake. I had to do something, so I looked towards the swing set, away from Mr. Nygaard, and hollered, "Run Teddy."

The hoodie guy looked in the direction towards the swing set, losing his grip on me.

I knew I had to act fast because there was nothing for him to see. I ran toward the swing set, where Mort was leaning against the frame with Teddy snug in his basket. But the hoodie guy was right behind me.

"Look you little ankle biter[26], I've had about all I can stand. Now give me the gun."

I grabbed Teddy as the hoodie guy grabbed me. I held on to Teddy as tight as I could.

By this time, Mr. Nygaard came out from behind the bushes. "Get away from de bairn," he demanded.

The hoodie guy spun round, "Well, well, well, if it isn't Pavel Lykke. You showin' up here sure makes my job easier."

Pavel? That must be Mr. Nygaard's spy name. I started to squirm within the hoodie guy's grip.

"Stop squirmin' or I'll put an end to ja." The hoodie guy was clearly annoyed. Mr. Nygaard took a step closer.

---

[26] Ankle Biters - Kids, tots

"Yup, this is my lucky day—first Disa and now you."

Disa? Oh, I'll bet that's Mormor Ohlson's real name. I sure was learning a lot.

"I won't even have to look you up later, will I?" The hoodie guy was acting all smart and tough.

"I vouldn't be so sure of dat, Lenny."

"Ha ... how'd you know?" The hoodie guy was clearly startled.

"Lenny, you quisle [27]... you traitor. Du may look like du ole man, but du nothing like him, dat's for sure. Ve know du killed him, didn't du Lenny?"

"You think you're smart, don't you old man? Well, the only thing you're getting' outta this—a pine box and lotsa dirt." He pulled a knife, while holding me tight with his other hand.

---

[27] Quisle – Norwegian for *traitor*

"Dat's de problem with hoodlums, dey're usually dumb as a box of rocks. Let her go Lenny, it's over."

"I don't think so. I saw you and Disa watching back then and I know she took my gun. I want it back now."

"Emma?" Mr. Nygaard said.

"She can't help you Pavel."

I looked at Teddy and Mr. Nygaard nodded. So I mustered all my strength and threw Teddy to Mr. Nygaard, who quickly scooped him up.

Lennie wrapped his arm around my tummy and lifted me. "I'm not kidding, Pavel—the gun ... now!"

And that's when I heard the growl. Before I knew what was happening, Lenny and I fell to the ground. He was screaming something awful. News now held him by the pant leg, pulling hard and shaking his head. Bernie was sitting on

Lenny's stomach and punching him for all he was worth.

Mr. Nygaard dragged me away and handed me Teddy. "Stay back," he said.

By this time, Bernie had tears streaming down his face as he kept pummeling Lenny. I heard sirens and tires screeching. Detective Haugen and Officer Klingerman ran over and started to pull Bernie away.

Mr. Nygaard grabbed Bernie, who was still swinging wildly. Officer Klingerman pulled Lenny up and placed handcuffs on him before he started to shoo the dog off.

Arnie jumped out of the police car and ran over to me. "Wow, I got to ride with the siren on. How great is that?"

TENDERMAIDS & SPAM

Mr. Nygaard took Bernie, Arnie and me to the Tendermaid on Waters Street to celebrate our victory. Before we left, Gosta gave News a nice big bone with some meat attached. We left him, locked in the store, gnawing away at his treat. I don't think he's going to miss us anytime soon.

A Tendermaid ... there is nothing better than a steamed Sloppy Joe-like burger and a milkshake: it's a real treat. I took my first messy bite and bits of steamed burger pieces fell back on the red and white checkered wrapping paper. Arnie was slurping his milkshake and making all kinds of nasty straw sucking noises. Mr. Nygaard rolled his eyes and Bernie ate silently.

My curiosity was building and I couldn't keep quiet any longer, I just had to ask, "Mr. Nygaard, you liked old lady Mormor, didn't you?"

"Yes Emma. Addie and I have known each other a long time. Ve met in de var and became quick friends, kind of like du and Arnie. Du know … playmates."

"So that makes you spy-mates then," I said.

"Something like dat. Du see Addie and I vere more dan ... mates." He stopped here, his eyes twinkled and he smiled before continuing, "Ve vere sveethearts."

"Ewww," Arnie exclaimed. "Did you have to kiss her too?"

"Ja, ve kissed too," and he gave Arnie a wink.

"I thought her name was Addie. Why did Lenny call her Disa?"

"Oh, ah ... vell ... dat's de little nickname I gave her," Gosta said.

"Did she call you Pavel?" I asked.

"Dat's not really important, is it?" Mr. Nygaard said.

I realized I wasn't going to get all the answers, but there were a few I really wanted to know about. So I reached into my pocket and pulled out the locket and handed it to Mr. Nygaard.

"Thank you," he said. He looked at it lovingly and then reached across Arnie to give the locket to Bernie.

"Wait," I whined. "Aren't you gonna look inside?"

"I know vhat's inside," Mr. Nygaard said. He nodded towards Bernie.

"It's a picture of you and your Mom, isn't it?" I asked.

"Ja, Emma," Mr. Nygaard said, answering for Bernie. "Du are right."

"So where is she then?"

"She got sick," Bernie snapped. Clearly, he was upset. He pushed himself away from the counter, his sandwich half-eaten. "I'm not hungry anymore."

Knowing it was better at the time to leave some things un-said, Mr. Nygaard turned to Emma and changed the subject, "I must say Emma dat vas one smart move, hiding a gun inside Teddy Snow. How did du think of it?"

"It was Teddy's idea," I said, rather proudly. "We knew we'd have to give the gun to someone and I thought Bernie could help us figure it out.

Until then, we wanted to keep it a secret. He's got a big pouch inside. Kinda like a puppet."

"Very nice," Gosta said, and then turned towards Bernie. "Ah … Bernie—du had better finish dat sandwich, boy. Du vill be needin' lots of strength a little later."

"Don't know what for," Bernie mumbled, but began to chew on the Tendermaid once again. And after his last bite, he gave Gosta a *I haven't eaten all day* look. With a chuckle, Mr. Nygaard promptly ordered another.

"Du know, Bernie, I've been thinking," Mr. Nygaard began slowly. "I'm getting a little too old to stack heavy boxes. I could use a strapping young man like du. How about stayin' at de store vith me?"

"It's too small there," Bernie responded, with a pout.

"Ja ... ja, du are right. But your Mormor listed me as her beneficiary. And I had her listed on my accounts, as vell. Ve vere sveethearts, don't ja know. Anyway, vhat's hers is mine and vhat's mine vas hers. So, I guess dat makes us, family. I tell you vhat; ve'll live in Addie's house and vork at de store. It's only about a fifteen minute valk. Vhat'd du say?" Gosta held his hand out for a formal hand shake to seal the deal.

Bernie nodded while trying to hide a smile.

As they shook hands, Detective Haugen burst through the door. He stopped and put his hands on his hips. After taking a big whiff, said, "Ah ... nothing like a good old Tendermaid." He shuffled over to the counter next to us. Once seated on the red cushioned stool, he said, "Hilde, a sandwich please. The aroma in this place could make anyone hungry, even after a full holiday meal." He smiled from ear to ear.

Without speaking a word, the waitress dipped her big scoop into the bin filled with loose steamed burger and piled it high on a bun. Once topped with ketchup, mustard, onion and pickle, she slid the plate down the counter, grabbed a Coca-Cola bottle and snapped the top off with the bottle opener that was fixed to the wall. Then she walked over in front of him, plopped the bottle down and placed her left elbow on the counter while holding her other hand out for payment.

Grumbling, he flicked off a few dollar bills and said, "Keep the change."

"Looks like my lucky day," Hilde said. "My, my, my, I'm getting rich faster than molasses going uphill on a cold winter's morn."

The detective ignored her remark, "Seems like we may have solved more than Addie's murder here, Gosta," Haugen said, his mouth full. "The gun Emma hid in that stuffed snowman had Lenny's fingerprints all over it. And it looks like the same murder weapon used in Albert Lea three weeks ago."

"Ja, I expected that. Du see, Addie and I vere dere. De man, Emil Jensen, vas Lenny's father."

Detective Haugen began to choke. "You ... you were there? You witnessed the murder?"

"Let's yust say, ve vere in town and happened to see a gun. One couldn't leave such a thing lying around, so ve thought you should have it. Ve vere going to bring it in de day she vas murdered."

"Let me get this straight ..." Detective Haugen began.

"Nothing to get straight," Gosta said. "I didn't see a thing."

"That so."

"Ja, dat's all."

"Did Lenny tell you who he's working with?" I asked.

"What do you mean Emma? You think there is someone else?" Haugen was getting his notepad out again. That could only spell trouble.

"Isn't there always someone else?" I asked. I wasn't about to get in trouble for spying on Lenny in his room. It would get back to dad, and boy, I was in enough trouble as it was.

The Detective furrowed his brow and then after a moment of silence, stuck the notepad back in his pocket. He turned to Bernie. "So where to now lad? Where's home?"

"He's staying vith me," Gosta exclaimed.

"Legally?"

"Eventually."

"Well, looks like I'll be headin' out now," Bernie said.

"Oh, I think not," Mr. Nygaard said. "Der are several cases of Spam to get on de shelves."

Detective Haugen licked his fingers after taking his last bite. He chuckled, shook his head, than looked at me. "Well then, what about you, Emma?"

I used my straw to stir the leftover milkshake. "After I get home, I'm grounded for a month. Dad was pretty mad when he heard I went to the park." My *it's not fair look,* failed to get any pity from my friends.

More by D.V. Whytes

Website: Whyteontherock.info

GREYSTONE MYSTERY SERIES:

- Prism Poison
- Cookie Crumbs, Green Eyes & Murder

INSPIRTATIONALS:

- Love Beyond Measure (Awarded the Nihil Obstate)
- Onions in My Ice Cream (*Coming Soon*)

TEDDY SNOW & EMMA RAE SERIES:

- The Case of Bittermelon & Peppermint
- Die, Die, Pumpkin Spy

SHORT STORIES:

- A Rose From the Dead (*Coming Soon*)
- Tentacles of Death (Greystone Mystery)

DIVINE DUSTING SERIES

- Clown on the Reef
- When East Meets West
- Tail of a Scorpion
- Life Changing Love

35803080R00063

Made in the USA
Lexington, KY
07 April 2019